Up for the Challenge

"Oh, come on, Doug! We could be cadets together and wear those cool badges in the hallway."

"We don't have a chance, Harry," I said. "You and I both know Mary, Song Lee, and Zuzu will get it. They're the best students."

Harry shrugged. "So? We can still try. Just think how neat it would be to walk around the halls wearing a star badge like the LAPD."

I had to laugh. Harry couldn't wait to be a detective for the Los Angeles Police Department, like Sergeant Friday on old-time TV.

Other Books by Suzy Kline

HORRIBLE HARRY
and the Hallway Bully

BY **SUZY KLINE**

PICTURES BY **AMY WUMMER**

PUFFIN BOOKS
An Imprint of Penguin Group (USA)

PUFFIN BOOKS
Published by the Penguin Group
Penguin Group (USA) LLC
375 Hudson Street
New York, New York 10014

USA * Canada * UK * Ireland * Australia
New Zealand * India * South Africa * China

penguin.com
A Penguin Random House Company

First published in the United States of America by Viking,
an imprint of Penguin Young Readers Group, 2014
Published by Puffin Books, an imprint of Penguin Young Readers Group, 2015

THE LIBRARY OF CONGRESS HAS CATALOGED THE VIKING EDITION AS FOLLOWS:
Kline, Suzy.
Horrible Harry and the hallway bully / by Suzy Kline ;
illustrated by Amy Wummer.
pages cm.
Summary: Selected to join the school safety patrol squad, third-grader
Mary quickly turns into a bully and classmate Doug suspects she may
be tampering with the book raffle.
ISBN 978-0-670-01551-1 (hardcover)
[1. Schools—Fiction. 2. School safety patrols—Fiction. 3. Bullying—Fiction.]
I. Wummer, Amy, illustrator II. Title.
PZ7.K6797Hnnr 2014 [Fic]—dc23 2013029863

Puffin Books ISBN 978-0-14-750967-3

Printed in the United States of America

1 3 5 7 9 10 8 6 4 2

Ring the bells that still can ring
Forget your perfect offering
There is a crack in everything,
That's how the light gets in.
—"Anthem," by Leonard Cohen

Dedicated with love to my five dear
grandchildren: Jake, Kenna, Gabby,
Saylor, and Holden

Special appreciation to . . .

My husband, Rufus, who listened and talked with me about this story and helped with the hard parts.

One of my oldest friends, Robin Kaer, who shared Leonard Cohen's wonderful poem with me. I'll never forget our teenage years—those great summer days writing together.

My granddaughter Kenna and my neighbor Lisa for their helpful suggestions.

Amy Rowland, librarian at Shelter Rock School in Manhasset, New York, for sharing her Book Fair Bucks program.

Karen Ecochard, teacher and advisor for the Safety Patrol Program at Willow Grove School in Hackettstown, New Jersey, for giving me the idea for this story.

The AAA office worker in Manchester, Connecticut, who told me about the days when he was first lieutenant in the Safety Patrol Program years ago.

My copyeditor, Janet B. Pascal, for her valuable work on this manuscript.

And Leila Sales, my hardworking editor, for her very helpful questions and thoughtful comments.

Contents

A Special Star

My name is Doug, and I'm in third grade. I write stories about my friend Harry, who can do some pretty horrible things.

Like tickle your armpits or dangle a snake in your face. Or snoop in our teacher's desk!

But in this story, Harry isn't horrible at all. He's almost perfect.

For one week, anyway.

How did that happen?

Well, it all started with a special star.

My class was in the library, and Mrs. Michaelsen, the librarian, was telling us about our Spring Book Fair Raffle.

"Each time you read a book," she explained, "I'll give you one pink raffle ticket."

"My favorite color!" Song Lee exclaimed.

The librarian continued, "In two weeks, during the Book Fair, we will have a raffle drawing in your classroom. If I pick your raffle ticket, you will win a free book. Each class will have one winner."

Lots of kids clapped. Song Lee, Mary, and Ida jumped up and down.

"I'm going to read twenty books," Mary bragged.

ZuZu raised his hand. "How will you know whose raffle ticket it is?"

Mrs. Michaelsen answered, "You need to write your name on the back of each ticket."

Dexter held up his army book. "I'm halfway through this one," he said. "Elvis was a sergeant in the army. Just look at this page of medals!"

Harry came over right away and pointed to one picture. "Hey!" he said. "My grandpa has this same medal!"

"How cool!" Dexter replied, sitting down at a nearby table to examine it. When Harry joined him, I did, too.

The picture showed a bronze star hanging from a red, white, and blue ribbon. Our third-grade teacher, Miss Mackle, looked over our shoulders.

"That's wonderful, Harry!" she said. "Your grandpa was a hero."

"He sure was!" Harry agreed. "He caught a hand grenade with his bare hand and then threw it away before his troop was blown to smithereens. He lost his left thumb though."

Mary looked at the medal, too. "Could you bring it to class and show us?" she asked.

I could tell she wanted proof.

Harry nodded. "I visit Grandpa every week at Shady Pines, his nursing home. I'll ask him tomorrow." Then

Harry looked up at the teacher. "What are these two words?"

"'Meritorious Achievement,'" Miss Mackle said. "Does anyone know what that means?"

Dexter and I shrugged. We didn't know.

ZuZu looked up from his history book on Lebanon. "I do," he said. "It means you are so brave you deserve an award."

Harry flashed his white teeth. "That's why my grandpa got this Bronze Star Medal. For meritorious achievement in the combat zone. Someday I'm going to get a medal, too."

Mary hugged her hair-styling book. "Fat chance," she muttered.

The Safety Patrol Cadets

That afternoon in Room 3B, we got a visitor. It was Mr. Ollie. He was the oldest teacher at South School, and always wore a snazzy tie. Today his tie showed a spider hanging from a web. Harry noticed it right away and put up two thumbs. Harry loves creepy things like spiders.

Mr. Ollie had two kids from the School Safety Patrol Squad with him.

They were both wearing bright yellow sashes and gold badges. I didn't recognize the girl, but I knew the boy. It was JayVaugh, my neighbor. He was a fifth grader and captain of the squad. When I waved at him, he nodded.

"Salutations, boys and girls," Mr.

Ollie said. "Today I have exciting news. We are going to invite three people from each third grade classroom to join the Safety Patrol Squad. We need more helpers to keep South School a safe and happy place. If you are interested, write and tell me why you'd like to be a Safety Cadet at our school. I'll let you know Friday who's selected."

Harry leaned over his desk. He wanted a closer look at JayVaugh's badge. There was a star on it!

"Whoa . . ." Harry drooled.

"Any questions?" Mr. Ollie asked.

Mary was the first to raise her hand. "How do you get picked?"

"You should be a good citizen," Mr. Ollie answered. "Be responsible, do your work, and be kind to other people."

JayVaugh was like that. He helped shovel our driveway during the winter, and fed our cats when we went on vacation. He even changed the litter box, and remembered to put our house key back under the tuna can in the garage.

Mary beamed. I could tell she thought she was responsible, too.

Lots of kids were interested, so after Mr. Ollie and the squad members left, Miss Mackle passed out paper to everyone. "Let's use Mr. Ollie's invitation to join the Safety Patrol as a writing assignment. Write about whether you would like to be a Safety Patrol Cadet or not. You can add a picture when you finish."

"I'm not doing it," I whispered to Harry.

"Oh, come on, Doug! We could be cadets together and wear those cool badges in the hallway."

"We don't have a chance, Harry," I said. "You and I both know Mary, Song Lee, and ZuZu will get it. They're the best students."

Harry shrugged. "So? We can still try. Just think how neat it would be to walk around the halls wearing a star badge like the LAPD."

I had to laugh. Harry couldn't wait to be a detective for the Los Angeles Police Department, like Sergeant Friday on old-time TV. Last Halloween, Harry even dressed up like him and wore a suit and a badge.

Harry didn't laugh at all. He just gave me an order: "Get going on that paper!"

I couldn't believe Harry was telling me to do an assignment. That was a first!

I Want to Be a Cadet!

SAFETY PATROL DOES MERRY TOYS ACHEEVEMINT

At two thirty, we shared our essays and pictures. Ida's was a good one. I liked her picture of a Safety Cadet walking a little girl to the nurse's office.

Dexter drew a picture of a cadet who looked like Elvis. "Being on the Safety Patrol would be like being in the military," he said. "And that's cool because Elvis was in the army."

Mary went next. She held up a picture

of herself with curly hair wearing a yellow sash across her chest and a copper badge. She wrote two long pages. I was glad when she finally got to the end: ". . . so I would make a courteous cadet for the South School Patrol."

Miss Mackle smiled. "Song Lee? Would you read yours next?"

All of us had to listen extra hard, because Song Lee's voice was so soft.

"I think the South School Safety Patrol does good things, but I could not be a cadet. I am too shy. I would not feel comfortable giving someone a citation for running in the hall or littering. I like the badge, though. It's very shiny."

"Thank you for being honest," Miss Mackle replied. "ZuZu?"

"I'm in Mr. Skooghammer's morning computer club," he read. "If I were a cadet, I wouldn't be able to do that. So I'm not going to apply. But I think it's great we have Safeties helping kids get from the buses to their rooms. I remember when I was a new student in December at South School, a Safety escorted me to class when I forgot where my new room was."

Harry and I exchanged hopeful looks. ZuZu and Song Lee weren't interested! Maybe we *could* get picked, after all.

"Harry?" Miss Mackle called.

Harry jumped out of his seat and stood tall by his desk. He unrolled three papers that were taped together like a banner. Everyone could see his block letters and stars.

SAFETIE PATROLL DOES MERRYTOYS ACHEEVEMINT

Mary rolled her eyes. "Harry is a horrible speller!" she said under her breath.

Harry read his essay. "I want to be a cadet! I want to wear a badge and be a Safety Detective. I'll keep everyone safe at South School. And if there's a crime, I'll solve it. I'm going to be very helpful and do all my work. I already know what the citations look like because I've gotten one for running in the hall. Please choose me. I want to

16

earn a star badge like my grandpa."

Mary covered her mouth and said nothing.

Song Lee and I clapped for Harry.

"Well," the teacher said. "I'm delighted you're doing your homework this week."

Harry flashed a toothy smile.

I shared my essay next.

"My brother, Baxter, is in first grade. If I were a Safety, I would make sure he and his first grade friends got to class safely. Sometimes Baxter thinks a person's rear end is a punching bag. He needs to be reminded about keeping his hands to himself. I have experience telling a little kid about the school rules because I have to live with

Baxter, and I help Mom when she runs his Cub Scout meetings. Being a cadet is probably not easy, but it's an important job. It would be an honor to be one."

When some kids clapped along with Harry, I felt good, but I still knew it would be a long shot for me to get in.

Harry's Perfect Week

Harry was a perfect citizen the rest of the week.

On Tuesday morning, he was the first person to hang up his coat in Room 3B. I know that because we just got a new hanger, a purple plastic one, and everybody wants to use it. All the other hangers are old wooden ones. When I got to class, Harry's leather jacket was hanging on that purple hanger, all zipped up.

Harry did every assignment, even the cursive handwriting lesson for capital "Q," which he hates.

When we had our morning meeting, Harry raised his hand. He didn't blurt out like Sidney. Harry picked up scraps off the floor and put them in the wastepaper basket. If he saw a crumpled piece of paper or crayon wrapper, he put it in the blue recycling bin.

On Wednesday, he volunteered to help Mr. Beausoleil, the custodian, wash the cafeteria tables. It was spaghetti day, so Harry had to pick up every sticky noodle under the table. I thought that was gross, but Harry said it was the best part of the job.

And on Thursday, when Miss Mackle asked for someone to straighten up the art supply closet, Harry volunteered again. He made all nine hundred crayons stand up in the crayon caddy, and sorted them by the colors of the rainbow, ROYGBIV!

On Friday, Harry brought his grandpa's medal to show during our morning circle.

"This is the Bronze Star," he said, holding it up. We all gazed at the red, white, and blue ribbon that was attached. The white part was yellowish. "It's very old and very special. When I asked my grandpa what it feels like to be a hero, he said he was just doing what had to be done. That's what a soldier does. I'm really proud of him." Harry dangled the medal in front of Mary's face. "He earned it for his merry-toys achievement," Harry added.

"You mean *mer-i-tor-i-ous* achievement," Mary corrected.

"Thank you, Mare," Harry replied with a smile.

Mary's eyes bulged. She seemed surprised that Harry was so polite.

When it was time for art, Mrs. Matalata twirled into Room 3B. As usual, she had a long, colorful scarf draped around her neck. "Boys and girls, did anyone remember to bring in a quote for extra credit today?"

Mary and Harry were the only two who raised their hands.

Mary went first. "'Treat people the

way you want to be treated,'" she said.

Mrs. Matalata clapped her hands, "Ah, the Golden Rule! We need to be reminded of that every day. Thank you, Mary."

Then she rushed over to Harry's desk and sat on it. "You have one too, Harry?" she said.

"My grandpa told me this one. It's real good." And he read it from a small piece of paper.

"'There is a crack in everything. That's how the light gets in.'" Then he added, "By Leonard Cohen."

"I love it!" Mrs. Matalata said, putting her hand over her heart.

Harry grinned. Mary made a face. I think she was a little jealous.

"There's more," Harry said. "I just read my favorite line."

*"Ring the bells that still can
  ring
Forget your perfect offering
There is a crack in everything
That's how the light gets in."*

Just as the art teacher began clapping, Mr. Ollie came into the room wearing a goldfish tie. "Sorry to interrupt, but I wanted to announce the three students from Miss Mackle's class who have been chosen to be part of the South School Safety Patrol."

Everyone turned pin quiet. Harry made prayer hands on his desk.

"Thank you to everyone who gave me a paper. If I don't call your name, I hope you'll apply next year in fourth grade. We'll have more openings then."

I crossed two fingers for Harry and me.

Mr. Ollie took a list of names from his shirt pocket. "The third graders are: Mary Schwartz, Ida Burrell, and . . ."

Harry and Dexter leaned forward.

". . . Doug Hurtuk."

That was me! I was so excited!

As the class applauded politely, I turned to Harry.

He was slouched down in his chair. His hands dangled to each side.

Oh, man . . . I thought. It was supposed to be Harry and me in the patrol, together. Harry held out a hand, but when we slapped each other five, it felt wimpy.

Mr. Ollie went on. "We are having a meeting at noon today in my room to welcome the new members. Please bring your lunch to Room 4A then."

"I wish you were a cadet too," I said to Harry. Harry nodded, then sank further down in his chair.

Mrs. Matalata wrote Harry's quote on the whiteboard with a black marker. "These words remind us that there is always hope."

Harry put his grandpa's Bronze Star back in its metal box and tucked it into his backpack. "Mary was right," he mumbled. "Fat chance *I'd* ever get a star badge."

The Sash and Star Badge

THIS IS A REMINDER TO FOLLOW THE RULES AT SOUTH SCHOOL!

At noon, Ida, Mary, and I took our lunch to Room 4A. Mr. Ollie greeted us at the door. His room had lots of science books and tanks of fish.

"Welcome, third graders! Take a seat and start eating. I just want to explain a few things and get you your uniforms. You'll be starting first thing Monday morning."

Ida and Mary squealed when they

got their yellow sashes. I liked the badge best.

The other third graders from Room 3A were excited too as we listened to Mr. Ollie talk about when we would be on patrol, and what the duties were.

"Mostly, you are going to greet people with a smile when they enter and leave the school building. The most important thing you can do as a cadet is be kind and helpful," Mr. Ollie emphasized. "But you also need to remind students to walk slowly and keep their hands to themselves. If they don't cooperate, give them a firm verbal warning. If you have to talk to them again, give them this white citation slip.

"If you have to give someone two

citations, report that person to me. I'll have a good talk with him or her in my room at noon recess."

Mr. Ollie asked all fifteen of the Safeties to stand up. "This is how you wear your sash and badge. Shanelle is a sergeant, Carlos is a first lieutenant, and JayVaugh is our captain. Your rank depends on how long you serve. You third graders will start out as cadets."

Then he gave everyone their assignments. When he got to us, he said,

"For the rest of the month of April, Mary and Doug will be patrolling the hallway from the library to their room. JayVaugh will be on patrol by the office if you have any questions. Ida, you have the first grade hallway with Shanelle and Lola. In May, you'll switch."

I liked working near JayVaugh.

Mr. Ollie gave us each a pad of citation slips. "You're on patrol for one week, and then off the next," he added.

After we watched a fifteen-minute movie about what the Safety Patrol does, we got to go outside to recess. Harry was pitching the ball in a kickball game. As soon as he saw me, he shouted, "You're on my team, Dougo."

I was glad Harry didn't hate me for making the patrol. He really was a loyal friend.

When Song Lee waved to the girls to join our team too, Ida and Mary shook their heads.

"We have more important things to do," Mary replied. Then the two of them skipped away holding hands.

I wondered if Song Lee's feelings were hurt.

When she went back to playing first base, I was glad. Song Lee wasn't letting snippy Mary spoil her kickball fun.

The Hallway Bully

On Monday morning, Mary and I stationed ourselves near the library. She was standing against the wall, next to the Spring Book Fair bulletin board. I liked the big flowers on it. They were made out of pink raffle tickets. Mary had her bright yellow sash on, and her shiny gold badge. I did, too.

I stood in the doorway of the library next to a bunch of pink balloons. It was ten minutes before the morning bell, and some kids were in the library, asking Mrs. Michaelsen for raffle tickets.

Miss Mackle stopped by to say hi. "If anyone from our class wants to put a raffle ticket into the jar on my desk, please escort them to Room 3B, but *make sure* they put their names on the back of every ticket."

Mary answered before I had a chance. "You can rely on me." She saluted.

Miss Mackle saluted back, then hurried down to the office.

When I turned around, I could see Sidney talking to the librarian.

"So, Sid," Mrs. Michaelsen said. "What was the secret name of that impish man who spun hay into gold for the miller's daughter?"

"Rumpelstiltskin!" Sid shouted.

"Yes!" Mrs. Michaelson replied. She handed him a pink raffle ticket.

Sid flashed it in my face then skipped past the bulletin board in the hallway. Mary was right there waiting for him.

"No running in the hall!" she called.

Sidney stopped. "I was just skipping," he explained.

"Skipping is a form of running," Mary scolded. "This is a warning. The next time you get a citation."

"A c-c-citation?" Sid quickly took off.

"Stop!" Mary called. "You're speeding again."

"But I have to go to the can, bad!" Sid replied.

"Well, take this with you!" And she handed him a white citation.

My jaw dropped.

Sid made a beeline for the bathroom. When he returned, he was walking, not skipping. But Mary still called him over.

"Did you remember to put your name on your raffle ticket?" she asked.

Sidney pulled out a pencil and wrote his name on the back. After they exchanged a few words, Mary grabbed his ticket, and Sid went back outside to morning recess.

As soon as she was alone, Mary took out an eraser from her pocket and erased something from Sid's raffle ticket. Then, she wrote on it in pen!

What is Mary doing? I thought.

Suddenly, ZuZu came dashing out of the library with his own pink raffle ticket. Mary caught him before he made it down the hall.

"You were running," she said firmly.

"No, I wasn't," ZuZu said. "I was moving quickly. There's a difference."

"What's your hurry?" Mary probed as she watched him scribble his name on the back of the pink raffle ticket.

"I'm twenty minutes late to Computer Club," he answered.

"I can take your raffle ticket to Miss Mackle's jar for you. I have Sidney's, so I'm going there anyway."

"Thanks," ZuZu said. "You're a helpful

cadet." And he walked quickly to the computer room.

Mary took ZuZu's pink raffle ticket and placed it in the palm of her hand. Then she erased something, just like before, and wrote on the ticket again in pen.

As I watched Mary walk down the hallway to Room 3B, I wondered . . . was ZuZu's name still on his ticket?

The Hallway Bully Strikes Again

Right after Mary left, my brother, Dexter, and his friend came to the library. They had books under their arms. As soon as they saw the balloons hanging on the door of the library, Dexter started punching them. "Pow! Pow! Pow!" he said.

"Hey, stop that," I said firmly. "You might pop the balloons."

Dexter looked at me, then my badge, and stopped right away.

Whoa, I thought. My brother actually listened to me! I liked being a Safety Patrol Cadet.

When the morning bell rang, students started streaming down the hallway to their classrooms. Mary was back at her post, ready for her first catch.

I spotted Harry and Song Lee right away. They were just stepping into the building. I could hear Harry's voice booming. "Bet I can beat you to the purple hanger!" he said.

Song Lee giggled as she and Harry launched into a walking race to Room 3B. Mary was there by the Book Fair bulletin board, waiting for them.

"Just a minute, you two," she bellowed.

Harry looked over, saw it was Mary,

and then continued walking on his heels to our room. Song Lee stopped immediately. She looked like she was going to cry.

Then Mary gave Song Lee a citation without a warning! *Unbelievable,* I thought. Song Lee hadn't even been running, just walking briskly. Song Lee took the citation and left. I could tell she was upset because she wiped her eyes with her coat jacket.

When Mary came over to me, I could hardly look at her.

"How many citations have you handed out so far?" she asked.

"None," I said. "I only give warnings. I can't believe you just gave a citation to Song Lee! She's your friend!"

"I can't play favorites," Mary said. "You race, I ticket."

Mary sounded like a Safety Patrol robot!

As soon as the second bell rang, and the hallway was clear, I headed for Room 3B. Mary was still waiting for a straggler to rush down the hall. When I got inside our room, I noticed Harry had his leather jacket all zipped up on the purple hanger. Harry and Dexter were looking at Dexter's army book in the library corner. I joined them right away.

"Guys," I whispered. "I think we may have a bully in Room 3B."

Harry and Dexter both looked up. "Who?" Dexter asked.

Before I could answer, Mary strolled in. "Someone didn't hang up their jacket, Harry!" she called out. The three

of us went back to see. Harry's jacket was on the floor, and Mary's was zipped up on that purple hanger.

How fishy!

"Hey!" Harry said. "I hung that up a long time ago, and I zipped it up, too."

"Well," Mary replied, "you obviously didn't do it very well. You also didn't stop when I asked you to in the hallway for racing! Here's your citation. If I catch you one more time, I'm telling Mr. Ollie!"

Harry gritted his teeth. "Thanks for the reminder, ol' Golden Rule Mare."

Man, I thought. Mary didn't know what that rule meant!

After she stomped away, the three of us boys huddled together. "I know who the bully is," Harry said. *"Her!"*

"It's Mary, all right," I said. "And there's something else. She may be stuffing the raffle jar."

"What?" Harry and Dexter replied.

So I told the guys how Mary took Sid and ZuZu's tickets and erased them and wrote something on them in pen.

"I bet it was her own name!" Harry said. "The LAPD calls that kind of cheating *defrauding*."

"I bet she is guilty of defrauding," Dexter said.

"I bet she is too!" I agreed. "We should tell Miss Mackle right now."

"Hold on, guys. We have to find out

if it's true first," Harry said. "We need proof. A person is innocent until proven guilty."

"All right, so . . . how do we get the proof?" I asked.

"I have an idea," Harry said, "but I need your help. Do you guys want to be detectives with me?"

"Sure!" Dexter exclaimed. "I'll wear my dark glasses. You two bring yours. We have to be cool detectives."

"Okay, here's the deal," Harry explained. "You must finish reading your library books tonight. My plan depends on it."

"That's easy," Dexter replied.

"Sure is," I said. I couldn't wait to see what Harry's plan was!

Harry's Plan

At noon recess the next day, Harry, Dexter, and I didn't play kickball. We were too busy working on a plan to catch Mary. The three of us went to see Mrs. Michaelsen in the library. She was eating some cottage cheese. "Hi, boys," she said. "Nice sunglasses."

We all smiled.

"We're ready to talk about what we read and get our first pink raffle tickets," Dexter said.

The librarian took Dexter's book and flipped through it. "Okay, name one medal you get for meritorious achievement during combat duty in the army."

"The Bronze Star!" Dexter exclaimed.

Harry clicked his fingers. "I knew that, and I didn't even read the book."

Mrs. Michaelsen chuckled as she handed Dexter a pink raffle ticket.

After Harry and I earned ours, the librarian said, "Good job, boys!"

Then Harry told us what to do next.

"Now, Dexter," he explained, "you write your name on your ticket in pen, and Doug and I will write ours in pencil. If Mare is really defrauding, she will just write on two of these. She can't erase someone's name in pen."

Dexter tipped his glasses at Harry. "Let's do it!" And he wrote his name, DEXTER SANCHEZ, in pen. I wrote DOUG in pencil.

After we finished, we went outside to look for Mary. She was playing jump rope with the girls and Sidney. Song Lee was jumping high in the air. I was kind of surprised Song Lee was playing with Mary since she gave her that citation. But, Song Lee never held a grudge.

"Hey, Mare," Harry said. "We have our pink raffle tickets."

Mary immediately handed the rope to Sidney. "Oh, let me see." She examined each of our tickets. "If you want me to put them in Miss Mackle's jar, I can do that for you. I have to go in early since I'm a Safety Patrol Cadet."

"What a good idea," Harry replied. "That way Dexter and I won't lose them during recess."

"I'll go with you, Mary," I said. "But you can take mine, too. I have to look around for my badge."

Mary grinned when I handed her my raffle ticket. It seemed like an unexpected bonus to her.

"I'll go inside with you guys, too," Ida said. "Lola and I are helping the first grade teacher with her safety bulletin board."

The three of us cadets went back in the building and walked down the hall to Room 3B. Mary and Ida got their sashes and badges out of their book bags. I took longer on purpose.

As soon as Ida left the room, Mary tucked one of the tickets into her tiny top jean pocket. She took out her pink eraser and placed the other two tickets in the palm of her hand. I watched her erase something on each one. When she was finished, she put her eraser away, and got out her pen. Very carefully, she wrote something on each one of those tickets.

Harry was right! Mary didn't touch the third ticket. It was still in that tiny pocket. Mary had to be defrauding!

When the lunch bell rang, Mary

and I took our positions in the hall-way. Moments later, she caught some kids bouncing a ball in the hall. While she was handing them a citation, I cornered Harry and Dexter. "She erased our names and added something else on just two of the tickets," I told them.

"Just as I thought," Harry said.

"All right," Dexter replied. "Now we have the evidence we need."

Harry held up a hand. "Not so fast. It is evidence, but it's circumstantial evidence. Not cold, hard facts. We don't know what Mary actually wrote on the back of those tickets. Doug saw her erase something, and write something. He couldn't see what she erased or what she wrote."

"So what do we do now?" I asked.

"We wait for the results of the raffle," Harry said. "If Mary wins, we'll show those tickets she defrauded to the teacher *after* the drawing. That's when we'll ask Miss Mackle for the jar and dump it on the moon rug. Everyone will see how many tickets have 'Mary' written on them in pen!"

"What if Mary doesn't win?" I asked.

"We have a private talk with her," Harry replied, "but we don't turn her in."

"She'll win!" Dexter exclaimed.

She'll win, I thought. It was just a matter of time before we had the biggest catch of all: the Hallway Bully!

The Morning of the Drawing

Day by day, the jar on Miss Mackle's desk got fuller and fuller with pink tickets. I knew how many I had in there: five.

Dexter had four.

Harry had two. One for reading a detective mystery, and the second ticket for reading that army book.

At least half of those raffle tickets had to have Mary's name on the back. She bragged about reading twenty books, and we knew she'd cheated on dozens of others. She had a fifty-fifty chance to win that raffle.

Finally, the morning of the drawing arrived.

This was our week off as cadets on the Safety Patrol. When the bell rang, and we entered the hallway, I spotted JayVaugh by the nurse's office.

"Have you seen Mary?" I asked. She wasn't playing jump rope outside with her friends as usual.

"Yeah, she's with the nurse now," he answered.

Harry and I exchanged a look.

"Maybe her conscience is bothering her," Harry whispered. "Today is the drawing."

"I bet that's it," I said.

Dexter added his two cents. "Maybe Mary thinks she might get caught, and this is a quick way to exit?"

"We'll see what happens," Harry replied.

Everyone in our class went inside Room 3B except me. I was thirsty and needed an extra drink in the hallway. When the second bell rang, Mary walked out of the nurse's office.

And then, suddenly, she ran to the girls' bathroom.

I lingered by the fountain to see what would happen next.

JayVaugh waited in the hallway, too. When Mary came out of the bathroom, she seemed better.

"Are you okay?" JayVaugh asked.

Mary straightened her hair. "Yes, I am. I feel much better now. I think it was that chili omelet I had for breakfast." Then she paused. "Why didn't you give me a citation just now?" she asked. "I ran in the hall. I broke a school rule."

JayVaugh looked at her. "It seemed like an emergency, Mary," he answered. "I'd have to be a creep to hand out a citation."

Mary didn't say anything. She just nodded slowly.

"Do you want me to walk you back to class?" he asked.

I quickly ducked into Room 3B. I didn't want them to see me eavesdropping on them.

As soon as I got to my seat, JayVaugh came into the room with Mary.

"Thank you," she said.

"Okay, see you around," JayVaugh replied, and left.

Mary slowly walked back to her desk. Harry was waiting for her. "I know who's going to win the raffle today," he said.

Mary didn't answer. She was in a fog.

"Mare?" Harry said, sticking his face in hers.

"Oh," she replied. "What do you want, Harry?"

"I know what you've been doing!" he said.

"What are you talking about?" Mary asked.

Dexter and I stood beside Harry. "We have been looking into possible raffle ticket fraud in Room 3B," Harry explained. "And very soon, we will show the results of our investigation. So be prepared."

Mary sank down in her seat. "Harry! You don't think I . . . could possibly . . . do something like that?"

Before Harry could answer, Mrs. Michaelsen entered the room. "Time for the drawing!" she sang out. "Let's see who won the Book Fair Raffle."

The Winner

Everyone watched the librarian take the big glass jar of pink raffle tickets to the front of the room.

"Boys and girls, just look at all the books you've read! This jar is full of tickets. Congratulations! You are a winner even if I don't read your name because you have been enjoying all kinds of good books these past two weeks!"

The librarian swished her hand in-

side the glass jar. Round and round it went.

All eyes were still on Mrs. Michaelsen as she pulled out one pink raffle ticket. "And the winner is . . . Mary Schultz!"

"I knew it!" Harry said.

Dexter grinned. "The Hallway Bully wins . . . for now."

Mary jumped out of her seat and smiled. She obviously was feeling much better. "Thank you! Thank you!" she called out.

"Do you know what book you want?" the librarian asked.

"I'm going to choose one for Room 3B's Reading Corner," Mary replied.

"How wonderful!" Mrs. Michaelsen

said. "Come down to the Book Fair with me and pick one out."

Miss Mackle clapped her hands and added, "Thank you to Mrs. Michaelsen for all her hard work, and to Mary, who is sharing her prize with us!"

The guys and I exchanged a look. Ol' Golden Rule Mare!

As we all clapped, the teacher carried the jar of names over to the side of the room . . . and dumped it into the recycling basket!

Uh oh, I thought. *There goes our plan!*

A King-size Oops

Harry headed right for the recycling basket. And just when everyone was starting their morning work, he pretended to trip over it. He fell to the floor, and dumped the entire contents over himself!

Miss Mackle looked up and saw him. "Harry! Are you okay?"

"A king-size oops," he explained. "I'll clean it up right away."

Harry was lying on the floor covered

with crumpled-up paper and piles of pink tickets. Dexter and I immediately began separating them from the trash. Harry flipped the pink tickets over like hot pancakes. It only took a few minutes to line them up in rows.

Now it was easy to see all the names on the back.

And that's when we discovered the truth.

Mary had rewritten everyone's name neater, in ink. She even put their last names on their raffle ticket. There were twenty Mary tickets there. But she had earned those.

Just then Mary returned to the room,

holding our new book. Harry went right up to her. Dexter and I did, too.

"I owe you an apology, Mary," Harry said. "I thought you were putting your name on the back of everyone's raffle tickets, but I was wrong. I had scribbled 'Harry' in pencil. You wrote 'Harry Spooger' twice neatly in pen for me."

"I forgot to add my last name, and you did it for me on all my tickets," I added.

"You're no cheater, Mary," Harry admitted. "I'm sorry."

Mary looked at Harry. "No, I'm not." She paused. "But you and JayVaugh made me realize something—I've been acting like a Hallway Bully. I shouldn't have handed out citations so quickly or taken your purple hanger. I rushed to judgment, too. I forgot the most important thing Mr. Ollie told us: a cadet should be kind and helpful."

Then Mary walked over to Song Lee and said a few words. Song Lee handed her the white citation in her desk. When Mary tore it up, the girls hugged.

Mary did the same thing at Sid's desk, but those two didn't hug. They shook hands.

Whoa! I thought. There was hope that Mary understood that Golden Rule after all.

"Want to look at the new class book I got?" she called out.

The title of the book was *The History of Hairdos*.

Harry and I rolled our eyes. It was a book about hair!

Dexter seemed interested though. "Is there a picture of a pompadour?" he asked. "Elvis has that hairdo."

"There sure is!" Mary said. "I'll show you."

Harry and I slowly walked back to our seats.

"I'm no cadet, Dougo." He groaned. "And I'm not much of a detective, either."

"What do you mean, Harry?" I said. "You uncovered the cold, hard facts. That's what good detectives do."

Harry glanced over at Mary and Dexter. They were still looking at that hair book.

"Well, at least we don't have to deal with a bully in the hall," he said.

And we high-fived each other.

Nighttime News

That night, I got a phone call. It was Harry.

"Hey, Dougo," he said, "guess what?"

"What?"

"My grandpa said I could keep his Bronze Star."

"No kidding?" I replied.

"No kidding," Harry repeated. "When I told him how things turned out with the Book Fair Raffle, and that I wasn't picked for the squad, Grandpa said I could keep it. He said it took courage to tell Mary I was wrong and to apologize."

"You *were* brave! I wouldn't have said a thing if you hadn't. And if you think about it, Harry, your saying sorry to Mary was contagious. After that, she went right over and said sorry to Song Lee and Sid."

"I don't know about that," Harry said, "but I do know I'm going to take good care of Grandpa's star."

"You will," I replied. "And you know what else I think?"

"What?"

"When we're in fourth grade, we're going to be cadets together!"

"I'm hoping!" Harry replied.